SESAME STREET

BIG BIRD
VISITS NAVAJO COUNTRY

By Liza Alexander
Illustrated by Maggie Swanson

A SESAME STREET/GOLDEN BOOK

Published by Western Publishing Company, Inc., in conjunction with Children's Television Workshop.

This educational book was created in cooperation with the Children's Television Workshop, producers of SESAME STREET. Children do not have to watch the television show to benefit from this book. Workshop revenues from this product will be used to help support CTW educational projects.

P9-CEU-497

Big Bird was waiting at a bus stop in the Arizona desert. He was excited. Big Bird's pen pal, Joey, was coming to pick him up! Joey was ten years old and an American Indian. Joey and his family belonged to the Navajo nation.

A pickup truck rumbled down the dusty road. Joey waved his hat and yelled, "*Yah teh!*" From Joey's letters, Big Bird knew that "*Yah teh!*" meant hello in the Navajo language.

Joey, his sister, Sally, and their father stopped on the way home to show Big Bird a scenic view.

"I'm so excited to be here with you all in Navajo country," Big Bird said. "We can herd sheep, and plant corn, and make jewelry and blankets, and ride horses—"

"Whoa!" said Joey with a laugh. "Slow down, Big Bird. There'll be plenty of time for everything!"

"Now it's time to look at the sunset,"
Sally added.

"Oh," said Big Bird. For the first time he
looked around. The sunset made the rock walls
of the canyon look fiery red. "Wow!" said
Big Bird.

In the summer Joey and his family stayed out in the country with his grandmother and uncle. In the winter they lived in the town where Joey and Sally went to school.

"*Yah teh*, Grandmother!" Joey said. "I'd like to introduce our friend Big Bird."

"Welcome," said Grandmother. "Come! Let me show you our hogan."

The hogan was a small round house made of logs and clay. It had thick walls and a chimney pipe on top. In the doorway hung a colorful blanket.

At dinner Big Bird met the rest of Joey's family—
his mother and his uncle Tony. They ate special
Navajo food. The night sky was wide and bright
with stars.

When she had finished eating, Grandmother said,
"Navajos have lived here in this country a long time,
long before it was called Arizona, long before there

was a United States of America. There are many
stories about our ancestors. Let me tell you one
about how the first hogan was built.

"In the beginning was a Navajo family whom we
call First Man, First Woman, and Little Boy. They
wanted to build a home, so they asked the animals
for advice.

"High on a canyon wall, Cliff Swallow said, 'My nest is built with twigs plastered with mud to make it strong.'

"Beside a stream, Beaver said, 'The roof of my lodge is round and sturdy.'

"On his anthill, Red Ant said, 'My door faces east so when I wake up I can greet the sun.'

"In her web, Spider said, 'See how I weave. If you weave, you can make beautiful things for your home.'

"So First Man, First Woman, and Little Boy built their hogan. Its walls were plastered with mud like Cliff Swallow's nest, and its roof was round and sturdy like Beaver's lodge. The door faced east to greet the sun, just like Red Ant's door. And in the doorway hung a beautiful blanket, because Spider had taught First Woman how to weave.

"And," Grandmother finished, "Navajos have been living in hogans ever since!"

Uncle Tony chuckled. "But nowadays some Navajos like air-conditioning. Good night!" Then Joey and Sally's mother, father, and uncle went off to their shiny new mobile home.

Later that night, inside the hogan, Big Bird, Joey, and Sally snuggled in their sleeping bags. Big Bird whispered, "Can I help you herd sheep tomorrow?"

Joey laughed softly. "Maybe, Big Bird. Let's wait and see what the new day brings. Good night, now."

"Nighty-night," said Big Bird.

When Big Bird awoke the next morning, Grandmother and Sally were in the garden, watering the corn. "Hi!" said Big Bird. "Where's Joey? We're going to herd sheep today."

"I don't know," answered Sally. "But he asked me to show you around, because he's out looking for a surprise for us."

On the other side of the hogan, Sally's
mother was weaving a blanket on a big loom.
The pattern was colored like the bright blue
sky and the canyon's pink walls.

"That's the prettiest blanket I've ever seen!"
said Big Bird. "When will it be done?"

"Thank you, Big Bird," said Sally's mother.
"I'm about halfway done now. It will be several
more weeks until the blanket is finished. Then I
will sell it. Weaving is my work."

Next, Sally took Big Bird to see her father in his silversmith shop. Quietly and carefully, he was crafting a beautiful necklace of silver and turquoise.

Then Sally and Big Bird went over to see Uncle Tony in the corral. Big Bird asked, "Did Joey go herding sheep without me?"

"No," said Uncle Tony. "Every last sheep is right here with me. You and Sally are just in time to help with the shearing."

"All right!" said Big Bird.

Uncle Tony gently cut the fleece from the sheep's back.

"The sheep is getting a haircut!" said Big Bird.

"This fleece will be cleaned and spun into wool yarn, then dyed," said Uncle Tony. "Joey's mother will weave the colored yarn into one of her blankets."

"Neat," said Big Bird. Just then Joey came by with two ponies. "Joey!" said Big Bird. "Where have you been?"

"Hop on this pony and I'll show you," said Joey. "Sally, you're invited, too."

"Look at that rock!" said Big Bird. "It's as big as a skyscraper!"

"That rock tower is as tall as the Empire State Building," said Sally.

"Now I'll tell you where I've been all morning," said Joey. "I've been searching for cactuses. Cactuses only bloom for a short while, and I didn't want you to miss seeing the flowers."

"Flowers!" said Big Bird. "We have flowers on Sesame Street. I wanted to see the stuff you told me about in your letters, like planting corn, and making jewelry, and weaving blankets, and herding sheep— Whoops, I did see all that today. Sorry, Joey. I guess I'm being impatient."

"That's okay," said Joey. "Now, Big Bird, take a look at this cactus flower."

"That's the most amazing flower I've ever seen!" said Big Bird. "Thank you both for helping me see things the Navajo way."